The Bubble Gum Kid

by Stu Smith

Illustrated by Julia Woolf

RUNNING PRESS
KIDS
PHILADELPHIA·LONDON

Text © 2006 by Stu Smith
Illustration © 2006 by Julia Woolf

Printed in China

9   8   7   6   5   4   3   2
Digit on the right indicates the number of this printing

Library of Congress Control Number: 2005932856

ISBN-13: 978-0-7624-2046-9
ISBN-10: 0-7624-2046-4

Designed by Frances J. Soo Ping Chow
Edited by Andra Serlin
Typography: Agenda and Jimbo

This book may be ordered by mail from the publisher.
Please include $2.50 for postage and handling.
But try your bookstore first!

Running Press Kids, an imprint of Running Press Book Publishers
125 South Twenty-Second Street
Philadelphia, Pennsylvania 19103-4399

Visit us on the web!
www.runningpress.com

For my three gum-chewing brothers, Steve, Scott, and Shawn
(and Dr. Frank Ferrara, thanks for the straight teeth!).

—S.S.

For Elsie, always my inspiration.

—J.W.

This is the story of Billy Bob Glum.
A wee, little tyke who oved to chew gum.

And because chewing gum was all that he did,
he was known around town as **"The Bubble Gum Kid."**

He once chewed a piece for seven straight weeks,
only stopping for meals, and to rest his sore cheeks.

Some say that Billy Bob chewed in his sleep,
and that even his dreams had gum-chewing sheep.

But, alas, poor Billy had one tiny trouble,
for try as he might he could not blow a bubble.

He'd blow and he'd blow till his face got all red,
but the gum would pop out of his wee, little head.

The school-yard bully, named Double Chin Dan,
wasn't exactly a Billy Bob fan.

He teased little Billy, popped gum in his face,
then tripped him to win the potato-sack race.

Now Billy Bob had about all he could take,
and Dan would soon learn that he'd made a mistake.

For Billy got help from his mischievous sister,
a terror of sorts that his parents called "Twister."

She taught him to blow and to pucker his lips,
and she gave him a few of her top secret tips.

With time little Billy became pretty good.
He blew the best bubbles in all of Mount Hood.

He learned to blow shapes, and animals, too.
His most difficult trick was "The Pink Kangaroo."

At night he blew bubbles inside one another,
a feat that impressed his gum-chewing mother.

So one recess 'Ol Billy came up with a plan.
He'd blow a huge bubble and show that kid, Dan.

He packed his mouth full of his favorite gum,
and in minutes all eyes were on Billy Bob Glum.

His bubble grew larger with each breath that he took,
and he managed to grin as Dan walked up to look.

The kids were all cheering, some screaming for more.
Double Chin grimaced, then stormed toward the door.

Now Billy Bob should have known better and stopped
when the kids began hiding in case that thing popped.

Then along came a breeze and poor Billy Bob flew,
right out of the school-yard and over the zoo.

He sailed past his house and circled 'round town,
clinching his teeth so he wouldn't fall down.

Birds became stuck, that gum was like glue.
Kites became tangled, and model planes, too.

Billy Bob panicked. This wasn't his plan.
Then he looked down and saw . . .

Double Chin Dan!

Dan steadied his slingshot and took careful aim,
fired, then screamed, at the explosion that came.

Pieces of gum flew all over the school.
One knocked Miss Flubman right into the pool.

Another glob landed on top of the nurse.
Her head became stuck inside of her purse.

The custodian ran out with a bucket and mop,
but he fell on a piece and hollered, "Please stop!"

The trees were all covered, the jungle gym, too.
A class of third graders was coated in goo.

Principal Chaney took Dan by the collar,
"You'll clean up this mess and repay every dollar!"

And whatever happened to Billy Bob Glum?
He had to wear braces, so he couldn't chew gum.

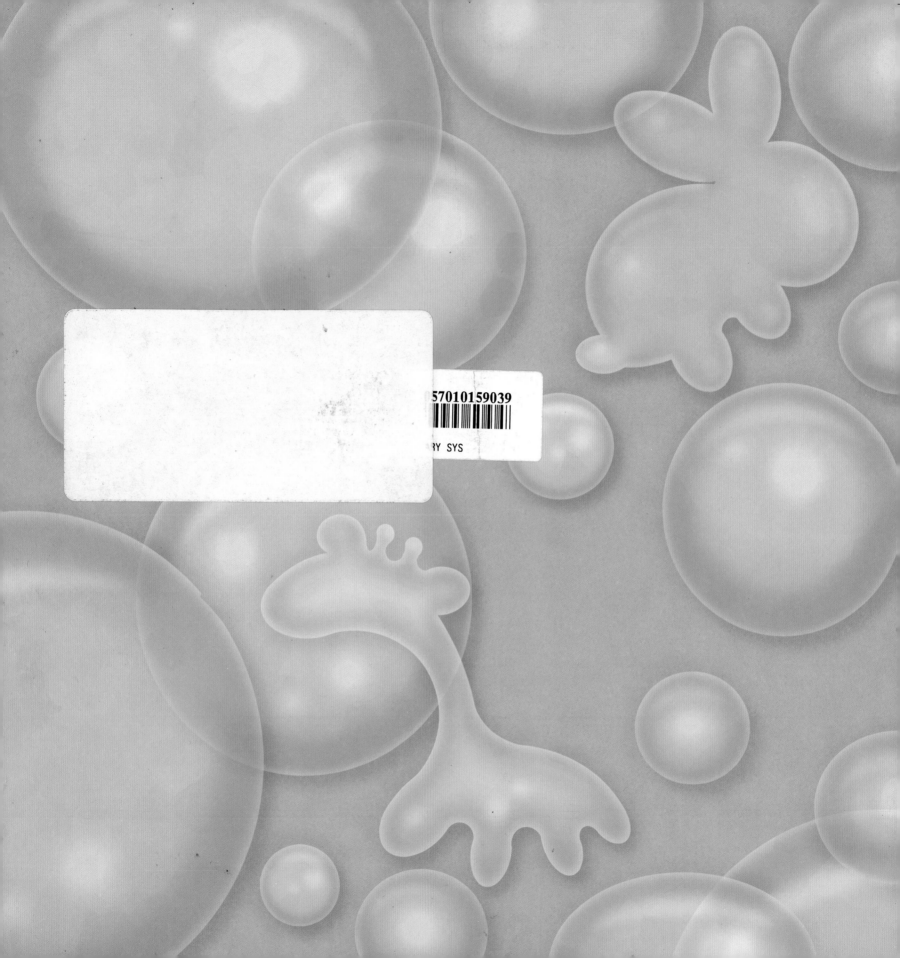